P9-DER-022

K

For the fathers and the sons
—A.D.

For Rudolph "Tito" Gutierrez,
my father, my friend, my hero,
Mr. Fantastic
—R.G.

Rayo is an imprint of HarperCollins Publishers.

Papá and Me
Text copyright © 2008 by Arthur Dorros
Illustrations copyright © 2008 by Rudy Gutierrez
Manufactured in China.

Library of Congress Cataloging-in-Publication Data
Dorros, Arthur.
    Papá and me / by Arthur Dorros ; illustrated by Rudy Gutierrez. — 1st ed.
        p.   cm.
    Summary: A bilingual boy and his father, who only speaks Spanish, spend
a day together.
    ISBN 978-0-06-058156-5 (trade bdg.) — ISBN 978-0-06-058158-9 (pbk.)
    [1. Fathers and sons—Fiction. 2. Bilingualism—Fiction. 3. Hispanic
Americans—Fiction.] I. Gutierrez, Rudy, ill. II. Title.
PZ7.D7294Pap 2008   2007011868
[E]—dc22

Typography by Dana Fritts
13 14 15 16 17   SCP   20 19 18 17 16 15 14 13 12 11
❖
First Edition

Arthur Dorros

Papá and Me

PICTURES BY Rudy Gutierrez

rayo

An Imprint of **HarperCollinsPublishers**

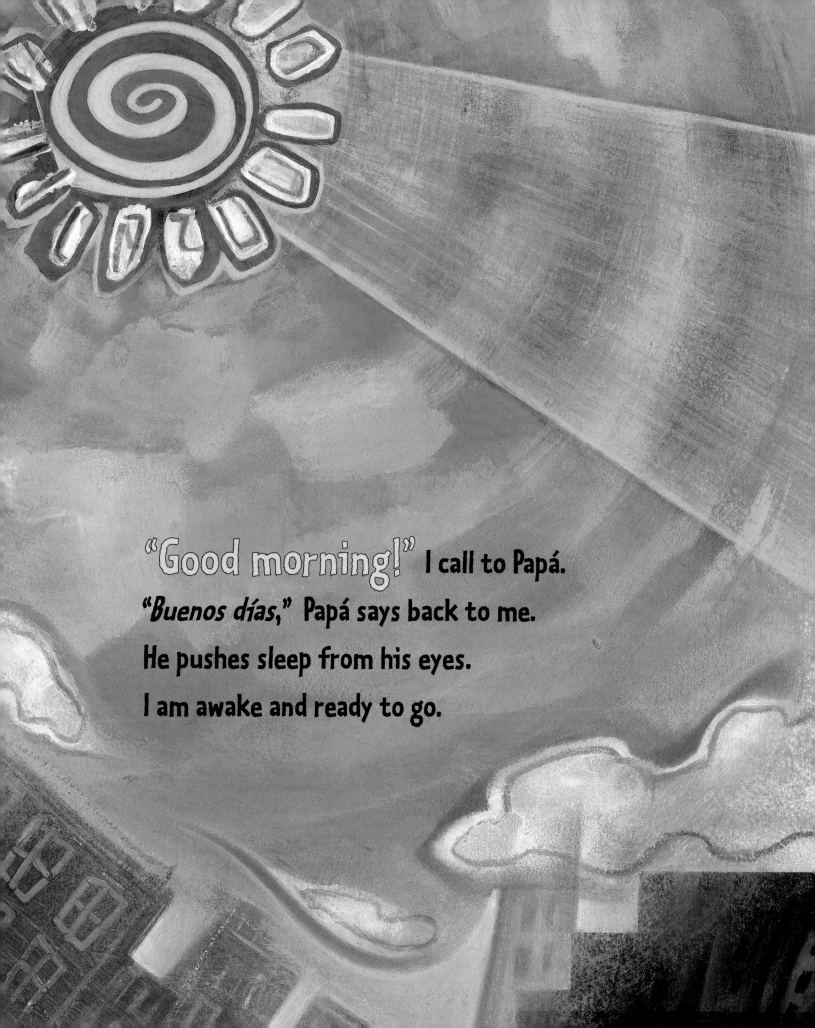

"Good morning!" I call to Papá.

"*Buenos días,*" Papá says back to me.

He pushes sleep from his eyes.

I am awake and ready to go.

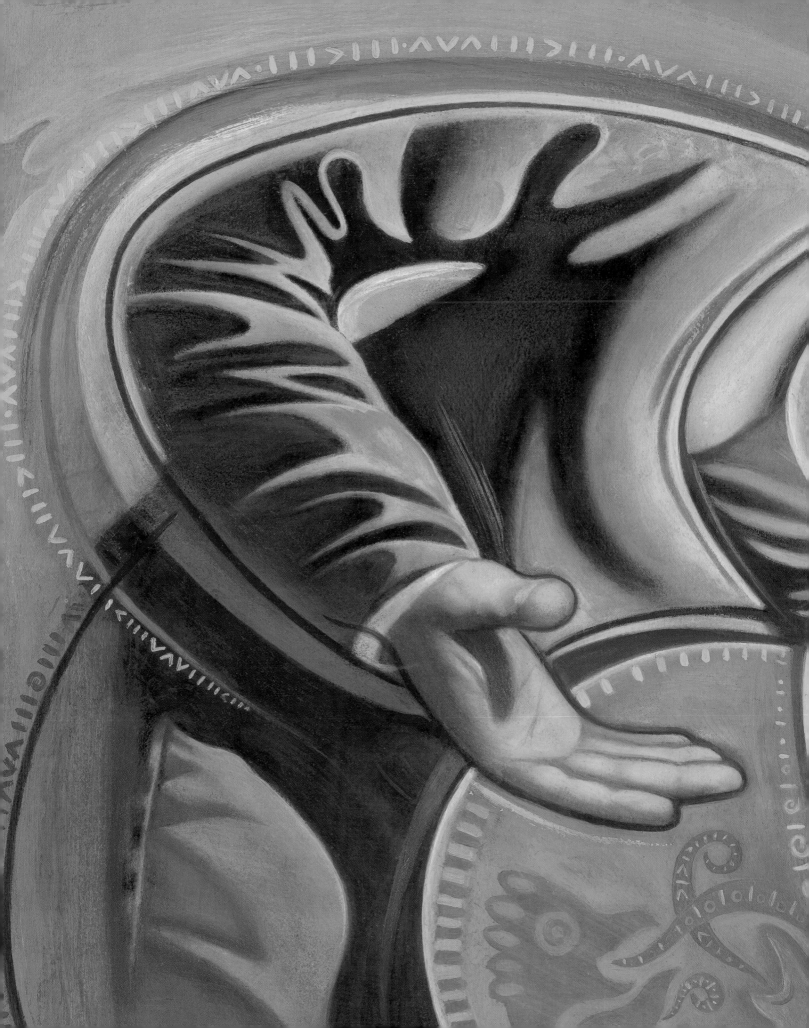

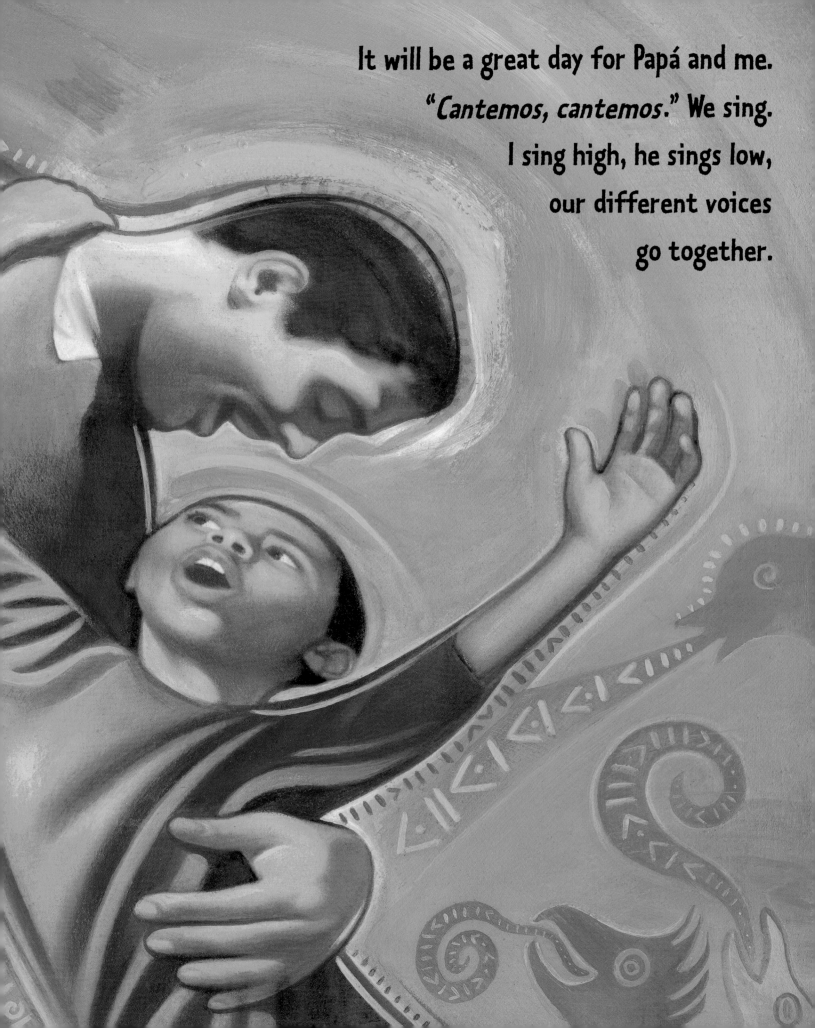

It will be a great day for Papá and me.
"*Cantemos, cantemos.*" We sing.
I sing high, he sings low,
our different voices
go together.

We are always cooking up something new.

He wants eggs. I say pancakes!

Papá brings down a plate.

He flips, I catch.

We invent a special food.

"*¡Sabroso!*" Papá says it is so tasty.

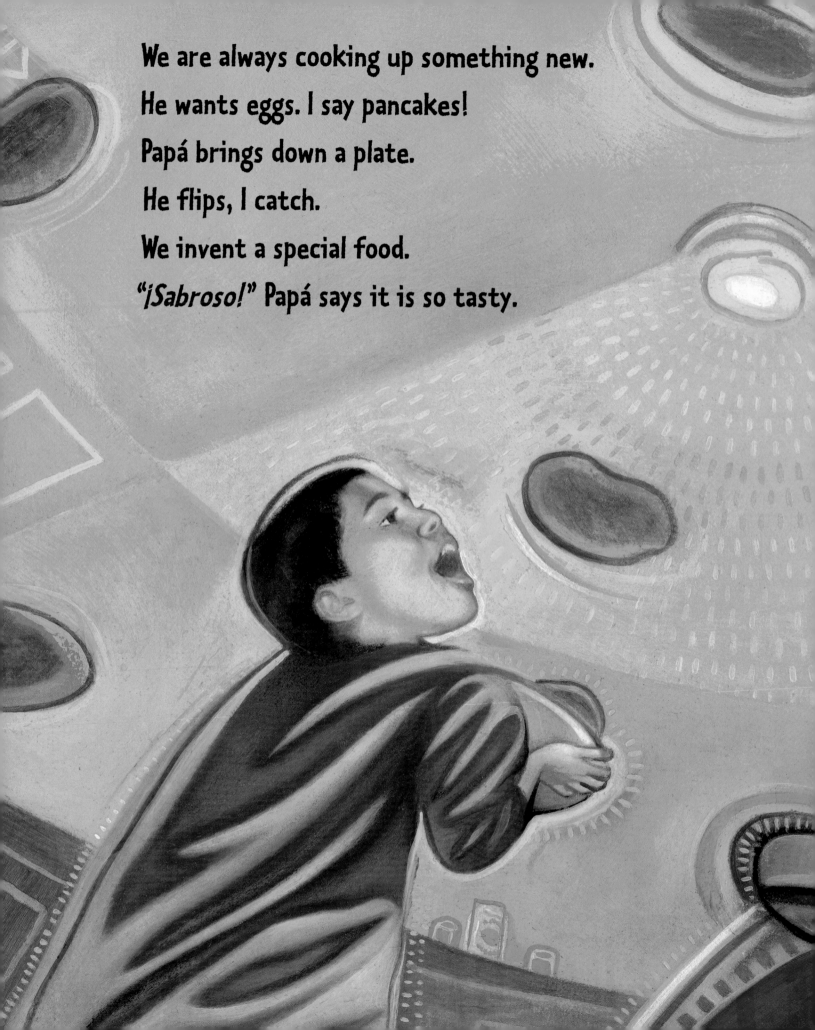

Today I know just where to go.
Crossing the street, Papá says,
"*La mano*," and takes my hand.
I have an idea. Papá has an idea too.

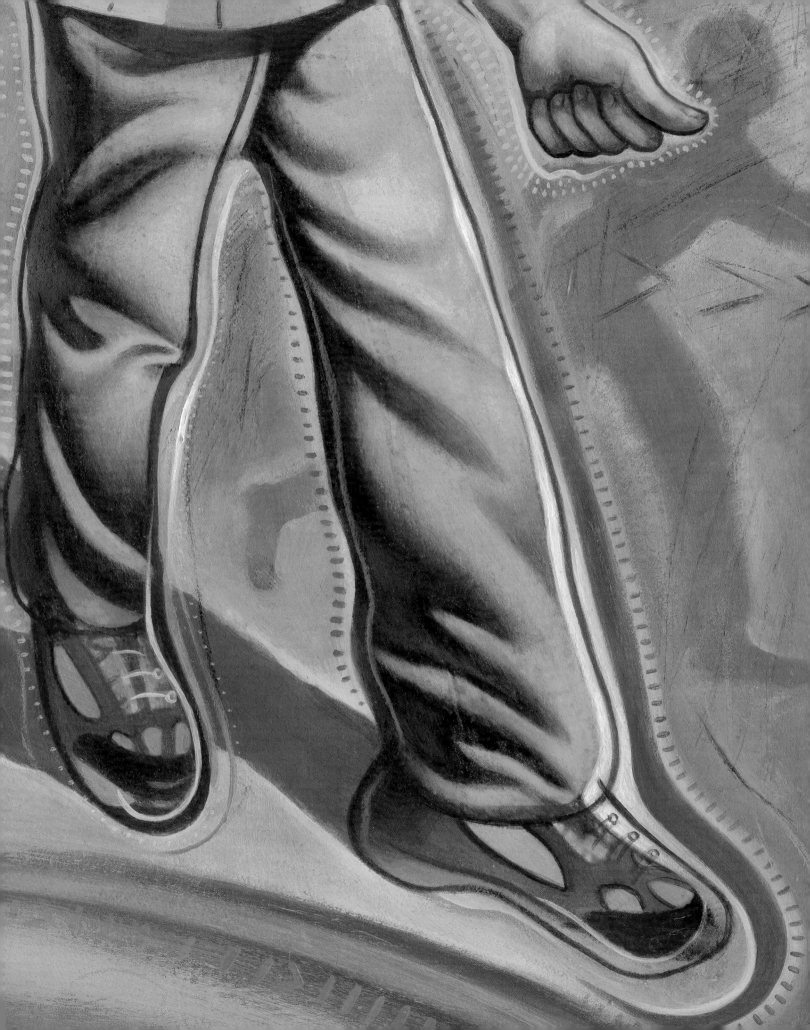

At the park,

I splash in puddles.

Papá steps around them.

"Agua Man."

"Water Man" he calls me.

Water here, water everywhere.

Papá swings me over.

There's a tree I want to climb.

I can't reach the branches.

Papá boosts me.

"*Alto, alto*, high!" I say.

I sway with the wind,

showing Papá what I can do.

I am flying, flying.

"*Cuidado*." Be careful, Papá says to me.

"*Mira*, look," I tell him.

A bird is up there.

"*Águila*." Eagle, Papá tells me.

He says my eyes see things he can't see.

In the sand,
I draw Papá's face. *"La cara,"*
he says, and draws me.

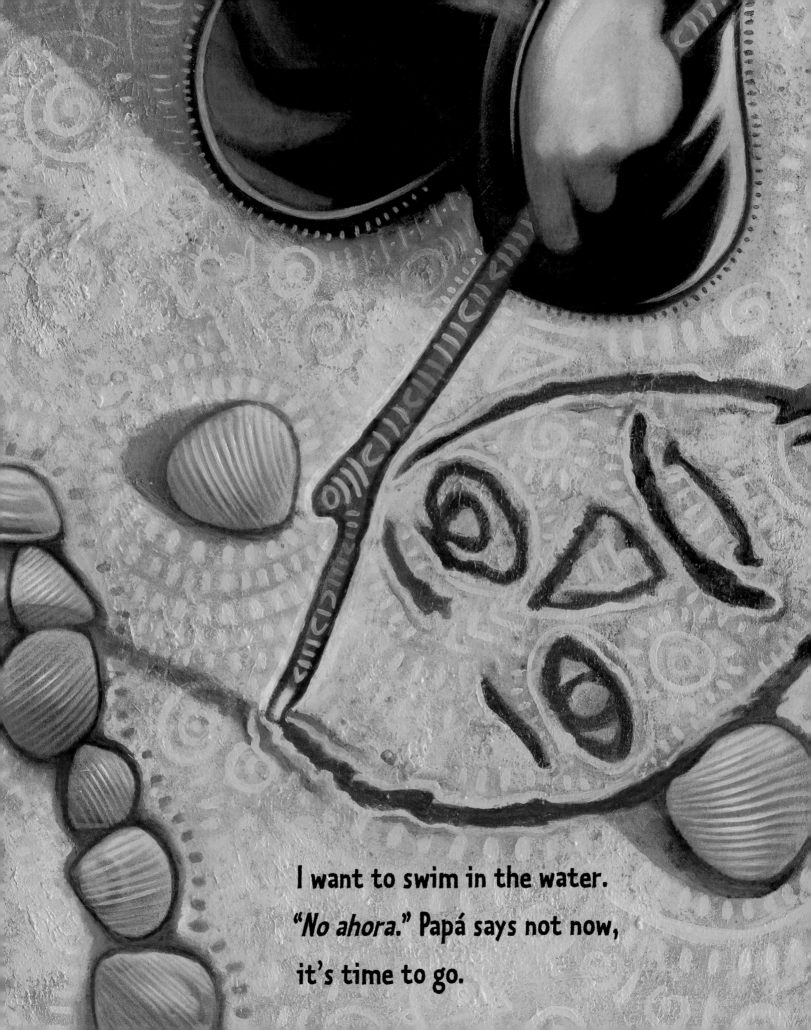

I want to swim in the water.
"No ahora." Papá says not now,
it's time to go.

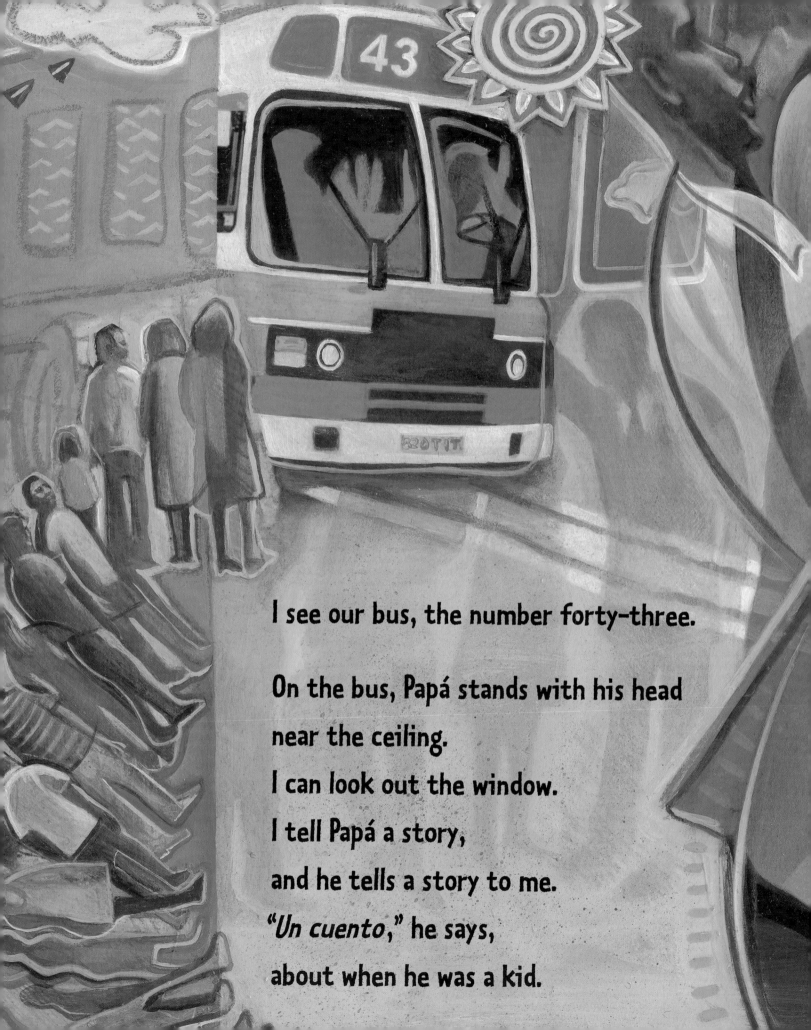

I see our bus, the number forty-three.

On the bus, Papá stands with his head
near the ceiling.
I can look out the window.
I tell Papá a story,
and he tells a story to me.
"*Un cuento*," he says,
about when he was a kid.

"Our stop, our stop!" I say to Papá.
I push the button and the bus
slows down.

Papá and me race the rest of the way.
I can do some things better than Papá,
he can do some better than me.

"¡Ganador!"

"¡Ganador!"

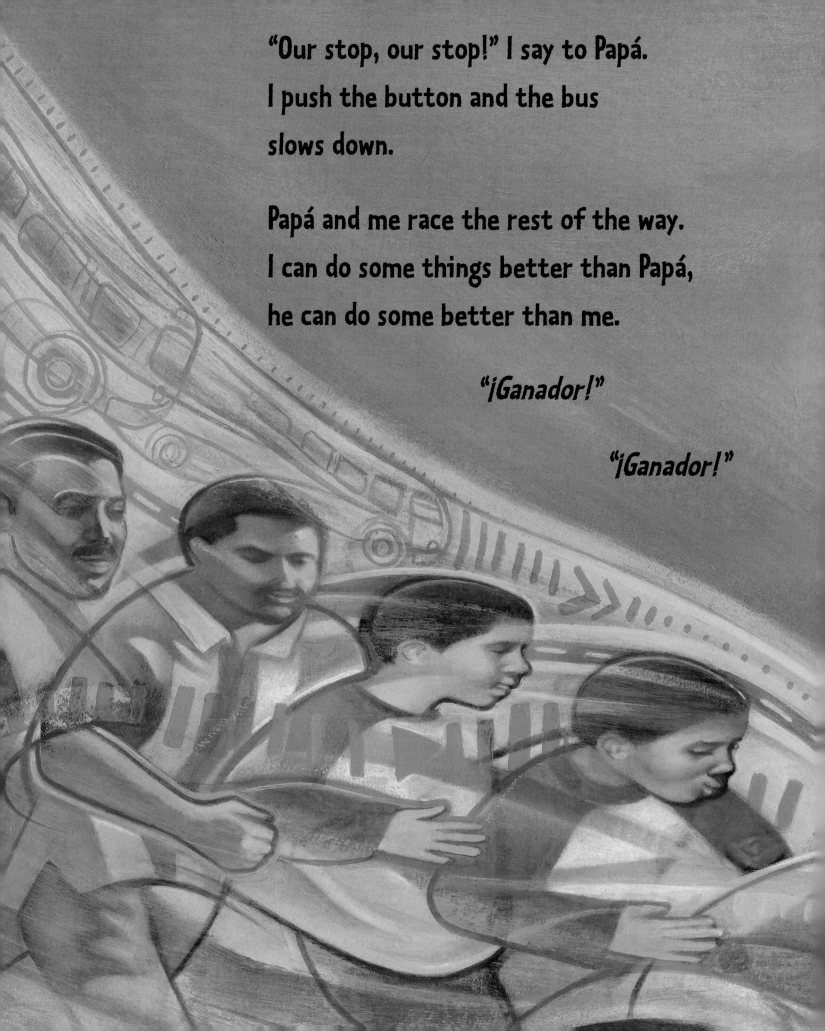

I knock on the door.
No one answers.
"*Otra vez,*" Papá says.
I try again.
The door creaks open.
Abuela and Abuelo,
my grandparents,
Papá's mother and father,
are waiting for us.
"*¡Abrazos!*" They give hugs
to me and Papá.